LA VAMP 2

LA VAMP 2

Angela Lartey

ISBN: 978-1-63901-441-5 (Paperback Edition)
ISBN: 978-1-63901-442-2 (Hardcover Edition)
ISBN: 978-1-63901-440-8 (E-book Edition)

Book Ordering Information

Best Books Media
132 West 31st Street, 1st Fl.
New York, NY, 10001 USA

www.bestbooksmedia.com
Info@bestbooksmedia.com
1 (347) 537-6903

Printed in the United States of America

ACT 1

Santa to Ash
What do you want for Christmas?

Ash
I'm 15?

Santa to Ash
You are never too old for Santa.

Ash
Can you just ask the photographer to take my cousin's photo?

Santa
As you wish, young man.

The photographer
Okay young lady, smile.

Photographer takes the photo.

The photographer
Here is your photo.

Ash
Thank you! Let's go Narnia.

Narnia
What about your photo with Santa?

Ash
We need to go Narnia.

They leave.

Monica
How was it?

Narnia
It was great!

Ash
I'm getting too old for this Santa and Easter bunny business.

Monica
It's part of being… <holds tummy>.

Ash
Are you okay?

Monica
Yes, I'm alright.

Ash
If you need to go to the lady's room, I will be delighted to look after Narnia and finish the rest of the Christmas shopping.

Monica
I can't give a credit card to a 15-year-old.

A female voice nearby
Touch me and I will call the police!

A male voice nearby
Since when did you become Wonder woman all of a sudden?

Female voice
Just go, Chas!

A male voice
You still belong to me!

Female voice
You have exposed me. That's enough to put a restraining order on you!

A male voice
I like to see you try because I can find a way to break that restraining order!

Narnia
Can we go back to the car?

Monica to Narnia
Why do you want to go back to the car?

Narnia to Monica
I don't feel comfortable.

Ash to Narnia
Just because you hear two people arguing, it does not mean you have to be afraid.

A male voice
Hay, where are you going? Do not walk away from me!

Female voice
I can go wherever I please!

A male voice
Not on my watch!

Female voice
Will you stop following me!?

Ash turns. He sees a girl and a boy heading towards him.

Monica
Well, what do you know.

The boy walks away.

The girl
Thank god!

Monica
How are you doing Annabel?

Annabel
Not so bad.

Monica
I can see you have done some Christmas shopping?

Annabel
Yes.

Narnia to Ash
Why are you blushing?

Ash
I'm just going to the men's bathroom. Be right back.

Ash walks away.

Monica
Is that Chas boy still bothering you?

Annabel
Yes.

Monica
My advice to you is that you put a restraining order on him.

Annabel
He will find ways to avoid having a restraining order put on him.

Monica
What do you mean?

Annabel
He is a psychopath.

Monica
Then have him placed in a mental asylum.

Narnia to Monica
Mummy!

Monica to Narnia
Yes, dear?

Narnia
Can you buy me and Ash a Christmas cookie?

Monica to Narnia
Later.

Annabel
Can I ask you for a favour?

Monica
Sure.

Annabel
Can you be with me until I leave the mall?

Monica
I have a better idea. How about we give you a ride home?

Annabel
That will be great! Thank you.

Ash returns.

Monica
Annabel is going to be with us.

Ash
Until when?

Monica
We leave the mall.

Ash
Really?

Monica
Yes.

Ash
Can I talk to you for a second auntie?

Monica
Sure. Excuse me, Annabel.

Ash and Monica go to a corner.

Monica
What's up?

Ash
Nothing. It's just that I like her.

Monica
But she's your elementary school friend.

Ash
But she has blossomed into a young adult girl.

Monica
Are you suggesting that you want to be her boyfriend?

Ash
Yes. But I'm a nervous wreck.

Monica
Do not be pressured to tell her how you feel.

Ash
Thanks, auntie.

They go back.

Monica
Shall we go?

Narnia
Yes.

Monica
Let's go.

They began walking.

Ash to Annabel
So, how is your dad?

Annabel
He's doing well.

Ash
Is Chas still annoying you?

Annabel
He's stalking me.

Ash
Is he?

Annabel
The other day I was at Wendy's with two of my friends from school, he came in and accused me of sleeping around.

Ash
Were these friends' boys or girls?

Annabel
Girls.

Ash
What a jerk!

Annabel
I wish he gets put away.

Narnia to Monica
Stop, mummy. The cookie store is just right there.

Monica to Narnia
I said later, dear.

Narnia
Please can we go in?

Monica
Alright.

They go over to the cookie store.

A man behind the counter
Hello there miss, what would you like?

Monica to the man
Yes, I would like two Christmas cookies, please.

Narnia
Make it four!

Monica
Okay.

Man
Would you like anything else?

Monica
No.

Annabel's phone rings in her jean jacket pocket, she takes it out.

Annabel on the phone
Hello?

Chas's voice
My tensions in getting you are high.

Annabel
Delete my number off your phone!

Ash
Is that him?

Annabel
Yes.

Man
Here are your four cookies. That will be $6.30.

Monica
Okay.

Man
Here is your change.

Monica
Thank you.

Man
Enjoy!

Monica picks up the bag.

Monica to Ash
Can you put this in one of the shopping bags?

Ash to Monica
Of course.

Narnia
Don't crush them.

Monica
Let's go, everyone.

The four of them walkout.

Monica
Let's begin shopping.

They walk away.

ACT 2

Doncaster
Do you just love Christmas?

Doncaster's father
No.

Doncaster
Do not be like that.

Doncaster's father
It is all a waste of time and money.

Doncaster
No, it's not!

Doncaster's father
People rushing about the place to get the best gifts for their friends and family.

Doncaster
This Christmas is going to be a good one.

Doncaster's father
You say that every single year.

Doncaster
Yes, but this year is going to be the best.

Doncaster's father
What do you have in mind?

Doncaster
You know that pink velvet box that I showed you?

Doncaster's father
Yes.

Doncaster
Well inside that box is a diamond engagement ring.

Doncaster's father
I was wondering when you and Monica are going to get married.

Doncaster
She is a wonderful woman.

Doncaster's father
Yes, she is. But can you at least wait until the twins are born?

Doncaster – I am not in any hurry.

The telephone rings.
Doncaster walks over to the table he answers it.

Doncaster
Hello?

A woman's voice on the telephone
Hello, is that Mr Mirandize?

Doncaster
Yes.

Woman's voice on the telephone
I'm calling about your daughter's dentist appointment.

Doncaster
Okay.

Woman's voice on the telephone
It has been rescheduled to January.

Doncaster
No problem.

He puts down the telephone.

Doncaster's father
Who was that on the telephone?

Doncaster
It was the dentist. She has rescheduled Narnia's appointment to January.

Doncaster's father
Okay.

Doncaster
Father?

Doncaster's father
Yes?

Doncaster
Can you do me a favour?

Doncaster's father
What?

Doncaster –Untangle the Christmas lights.

Doncaster's father
I'm not spending 2 to 4 hours untangling Christmas lights!

Doncaster
Please, father.

Doncaster's father
Alright.

Doncaster
Thank you.

Doncaster's father looks in the large box beside his armchair.

Doncaster's father
It's like Las Vegas in this box!

Doncaster
Whatever do you mean?

Doncaster's father
There's too many of them!

Doncaster
I will help you.

Doncaster's father
Thank you.

Doncaster walks over to his father.

Doncaster
Remind me to run you a bath tonight. You're starting to smell a bit.

Doncaster's father
I smell fine!

Doncaster to his father
Put your arm up.

Doncaster's father
Do not talk to me as if I'm a pre-teen!

Doncaster to his father
Lift them?

Doncaster's father
Fine!

Doncaster
Yep, you most definitely need a bath.

Doncaster's father
Scornful brat!

Doncaster
It is my duty to care.

Doncaster's father
What?! By sniffing my armpits like a dog!

He put his arm down.

Doncaster
I was thinking of teaching Ash how to drive.

Doncaster's father
The boy just turned 15!

Doncaster
I just think it's the right time for me to do so.

Doncaster's farther
Do not be like those families that buy cars for their children on their 16th birthday.

Doncaster
Why not?

Doncaster's father
I just think it's too overrated.

Doncaster
What is?

Doncaster's father
Teaching a child how to drive at 15 and getting them a car at 16.

Doncaster
Then what age should I teach Ash to drive?

Doncaster's father
When he's ready.

Doncaster
Alright, if you say so.

Keys rattling, the front door opens.

Tony
Hallo everyone!

Doncaster
Hello, Tony.

Doncaster's father
How is your girlfriend?

Tony
She's alright.

Doncaster
When are we going to see her?

Tony
She still a little shy in coming here.

Doncaster's father
Does she not like vampires?

Tony
If she didn't, then I will not be with her.

Doncaster
So, you already told her?

Tony
Yes,

Tony closes the front door.

Doncaster's father
Then, why is she uncomfortable in coming here?

Tony
Her self-confidence is not that great.

Doncaster
What do you mean?

Tony
She is a little on the plump side.

Doncaster's father
So, she is an average size female.

Doncaster
Why is she uncomfortable with herself?

Tony
It's a phrase she has been having since she was in high school.

Doncaster – Oh.

Doncaster's father
Is she seeing anyone?

Tony
What do you mean?

Doncaster
Is your girlfriend seeing a specialist?

Tony
I don't want to upset her.

Doncaster
Alright. Talk to her when you are ready.

Tony
So, where are Auntie, Ash, and Narnia?

Doncaster
They are out Christmas shopping.

Tony
Ah, good! I can get started on the Mince pies.

Doncaster's father
Do not put too much icing sugar on them.

Tony
I won't.

Doncaster
Hay Tony?

Tony
Yes, uncle?

Doncaster
Have you thought of getting a baking job?

Tony
No, why?

Doncaster
Just asking.

Tony
The world of work is not ready for someone like me.

Doncaster
But, you have talent.

Tony
Yes, but we live in a cruel world.

Doncaster's father
It's the people.

Doncaster
At least give it a try?

Tony
Nah, I'm alright.

Doncaster
Can you at least think about it?

Doncaster's father
The boy said no!

Tony's phone rings in his jacket pocket.

Tony on the phone
Hello?

Nancie's voice
Hate comments online!

Tony
What kind of hate comments?

Nancie's voice
The usual fat, ugly and some comments about you.

Tony
One's about me?

Nancie's voice – Yes.
Tony
What are they saying?

Nancie's voice
You want to know?

Tony
Yes.

Nancie's voice
Here is one of them. "*That hottie must be on drugs or blind to find a fatty like you attractive.*"

Tony
Go on?

Nancie's voice
Here is another. "*I envy the fact that someone like you could have a boyfriend like that. He must be mad.*"

Tony
Anymore?

Nancie's voice
"Death to the elephant. Hashtag take the boyfriend."

Tony
Okay?

Nancie's voice
"*What is he smoking to be with you?*"

Tony
Right, last one?

Nancie's voice
"*He's under a spell! Hashtag God save his soul.*"

Tony (laughs)
That is not true.

Nancie's voice
What are you up to?

Tony
I'm just about to make some mince pies.

Nancie's voice
How nice! Save me a few.

Tony
I will.

Doncaster's father
Dun it!

Doncaster
What's wrong father?

Doncaster's father
A bulb has come off!

Doncaster
Do not worry about it.

Tony
Do you want to do something in the New year?

Nancie's voice
Like what?

Tony
Does a weekend stay in Disneyland sound good?

Nancie's voice
Do you have the money?

Tony
Yes.

Nancie's voice
I love to spend a weekend at Disneyland with you.

Tony
Wonderful!

Nancie's voice
How are your brother and cousin?

Tony
They're fine.

Nancie's voice
Good. Anyway I must go.

Tony – Bye, dear.

Tony puts his phone back in the jacket pocket.

Doncaster to Tony
I'm guessing you will not be here to welcome in the New Year?

Tony to Doncaster
I guess you can say that.

Doncaster
I'm hurt.

ACT 3

Nancie
I'm going to Disneyland with my boyfriend.

Nancie's mum
When?

Nancie
In the New year!

Nancie's mum
When was this arranged?

Nancie
Just now!

Nancie's mum
You're not going anywhere!

Nancie
Mum!

Nancie's mum
I don't even like the idea of you having a boyfriend.

Nancie
Why's that?

Nancie's mum
You're not ready for that kind of commitment.

Nancie
I'm 21!

Nancie's mum
I don't care!

Nancie's sister Chelsea appears.

Chelsea
What's going on?

Nancie's mum
Your sister agreed to go away with her boyfriend.

Chelsea
To where?

Nancie's mum
Disneyland!

Chelsea
For how long?

Nancie
For a weekend!

Chelsea
No way!

Nancie
Why are you both so against my boyfriend?

Chelsea
It's not that we are against him.

Nancie's mum
We just don't like the fact of you going away with him.

Chelsea
Try not to be upset, but you are not fit enough to take that step.

Nancie
I'm so fit enough to take that step!

Nancie's mum
You get panicky when people look at you.

Nancie
It's a habit that I have been tackling since high school.

Chelsea
That is why you are not fit to go anywhere.

Nancie
It's Disneyland California, not Orlando!

Chelsea
Still, you are not fit.

Nancie's mum
Nancie, we love you, but you need to understand.

Nancie
Understand what?

Chelsea
About your situation.

Nancie
I understand.

Nancie's mum
Let's move away from this topic, and talk about something else?

Nancie
Fine.

Chelsea
Are people online still saying trash about you?

Nancie
Everyday, non-stop.

Nancie's mum
Why are you even on Facebook and Instagram?

Nancie
To get friends.

Chelsea
There are other ways to make friends than going online.

Nancie
I'm not a social butterfly like you!

Chelsea
You do not have to be an expert.

Nancie
Yes, you do!

Chelsea
Here is an idea. How about one Friday night, we go to a social club?

Nancie
A social club?

Chelsea
Yes.

Nancie
No way!

Chelsea
Why not?

Nancie
The last thing I want is some old guy asking me to be his friend.

Chelsea
You do not have to accept.

Nancie
Fine.

Chelsea
Wonderful.

Nancie
Do I have to dress in a certain way?

Chelsea
No.

Nancie
Okay.

Nancie's mum
I will get lunch ready.

She then walks away.

Nancie
This social club does it have a dance hall?

Chelsea
Yes.

Nancie
Does it have a VIP section?

Chelsea
Yes.

Nancie
What about a restaurant and bar?

Chelsea – Yes.

Nancie
Right.

Chelsea
Now, all we have to do is decide when we want to go.

Nancie
The Friday after Christmas.

Chelsea
That is too soon. How about the first Friday of January?

Nancie
That will be fine.

Chelsea
Good. Mark it on your calendar.

Nancie's mum
Lunch is ready.

Chelsea
Wonderful.

The two of them walk over to the dining table.

Nancie
It seems only yesterday that we cremated dad.

Nancie's mum
I know.

Chelsea
Are we doing anything to mark his 4-year passing?

Nancie's mum
Not this year.

Nancie
Why does it have to be cancer and not natural causes?

Chelsea
He did not deserve to die that way.

Nancie
It gets to show that there is no one looking down at us.

Nancie's mum
Do not say things like that!

Nancie
Dad was a good man.

Nancie's mum
Can we stop talking about him?

Nancie and Chelsea
Okay.

Chelsea
When are we going to do Christmas shopping?

Nancie's mum
This Saturday.

Nancie
Can we get a gingerbread house?

Nancie's mum
Sure.

Chelsea
It has to be a small gingerbread house.

Nancie
What about a chocolate log?

Nancie's mum
I'm not spending money on sweets.

Nancie
But, its Christmas!

Nancie's mum
Yes.

Nancie
So, treat the family.

Chelsea
Christmas is not about eating and drinking.

Nancie
Yes, it is!

Chelsea
I think you are old enough to understand that not everyone has a good Christmas.

Nancie
What people?

Chelsea
The elderly, poor and the homeless.

Nancie
Have the poor heard of a job?

Chelsea
Not everyone has the skills or the grades to get a job.

Nancie
Who asked them to drop out of school!

Chelsea
Maybe we should talk about something else.

Nancie
Yeah, we should.

Chelsea
So, have you thought about learning to drive?

Nancie
Yes.

Chelsea
If you need any help with payments, I'm willing to give you some money.

Nancie
Do not waste your hard-earned money on me!

Chelsea
But I insist on spending some money on you.

Nancie
It's okay.

Nancie's mum
You're a very nice older sister Chelsea.

Chelsea
Thanks.

Nancie's mum
Do not mention it.

Nancie to Chelsea
How is work?

ACT 4

Caroline
Where is he?

Girl 4
I'm sure Chas is on his way.

Caroline
We are supposed to be boyfriend and girlfriend!

Girl 2
I can see a blue SUV coming towards the house.

Caroline
Finally.

Caroline and the girls walk towards the SUV.

Caroline to Chas
Where have you been?

Chas
Can a guy have a social life?

Caroline
Just take us to the party!

One of the girls slides open the door.

Girl 1
Why is there a rope, handcuffs, a gag and a mask?

Chas (yells)
Just get in the car!

Girl 1
Alright no need to be angry.

The four girls get into the SUV.

Chas
Shut the door!

The SUV drives away.

Chas to Caroline
I think we should get intermit?

Caroline
I'm not ready to go that step further.

Chas
Don't be such a child!

Caroline
Just because I said no does not mean I'm a loser.

Chas
I did not say that!

Caroline
You just called me a child!

Chas
Is that what you are?

Caroline
Change the subject.

Girl 1
I feel uneasy?

Girl 3
Stop looking at them!

Girl 1
How can I?

Girl 2
Maybe you will feel better when we're at the party.

Girl 1
It's the sort of equipment that is used by predators.

Girl 4
Are you saying that Chas is weird?

Girl 1
No.

Girl 3
Then, stop thinking about them.

Chas talking
Yes, we are on our way.

A male voice
Okay, see you later.

Chas to Caroline
Why did you not say hi?

Caroline
Was I supposed to?

Chas
What is wrong with you?

Caroline
Nothing.

Chas
Then, cheer up.

Caroline
What do you want for Christmas?

Chas
You to say that you are ready to make love to me?

Caroline
No way!

Chas
Why are you afraid?

Caroline
I'm not afraid of anything!

Chas
How about this? If you make love to me, I will fund half of your College fees.

Caroline
I'm not going to college.

Chas
Why's that?

Caroline
My grades are not up to college standard.

Chas
What do you mean?

Caroline
I did not know being popular came with a good grade tag.

Chas
Are you saying that you are not smart?

Caroline
It is not my fault.

Chas
What about your friends? Are they stupid too?

Caroline
No.

Chas
After Christmas, I'm going to be your tutor.

Caroline
Please don't do that!

Chas
I'm not having my girlfriend work at some fast-food joint when she graduates from high school!

Caroline
Fine. How much do you want me to pay?

Chas
It's free.

The SUV arrives outside a mansion.

Boy
You're just in time.

The door slides open the four girls step out.

The boy
You girls look great!

The four girls
Thanks.

Boy
Would you like me to escort you all to the mansion?

Girl 4
We are fine.

The four girls walk over to the mansion.

Chas
Can you leave the two of us alone for a few minutes?

Boy
Sure.

The boy walks over to the mansion.

Chas to Caroline
Do you have a camera on your laptop or desktop?

Caroline
Yes, why?

Chas
So if I cannot tutor you in person, I can always tutor you online.

Caroline
Okay.

Chas puts his hand on Caroline's thigh, he slowly leans towards her. She opens the door.

Chas
What the hell!

Caroline
See you at the mansion.

She shuts the door.

ACT 5

Monica on the phone
I have finished.

Doncaster's voice
Did you get everything you need?

Monica
Yes.

Doncaster's voice
I got a phone call from the dentist.

Monica
Alright.

Doncaster's voice
She has rescheduled Narnia's appointment to January.

Monica
That's fine.

Doncaster's voice
Tony is making mince pies.

Monica
Is he?

Doncaster's voice
Yes.

Monica
That is one job ticked off my to-do list.

Doncaster's voice
Anyway, I must go before my father gets even more annoyed with the Christmas lights.

Monica
Okay.

Doncaster's voice
See you when you get home.

Monica
Bye, dear.

She puts the phone away.

Monica to the children
I bet you guys are hungry?

Ash
Yes, auntie.

Annabel
Can we go to a Japanese restaurant?

Monica
Let's go to Wendy's instead.

She closes the boot.

Monica
Okay children, into the car you go.

They walk to the side of the car.
Ash opens the door.

Ash to Annabel
After you.

Annabel steps into the car, followed by Narnia.

Ash
To the car seat you go, Narnia.

Annabel
Would you like me to put her seat belt on?

Ash
That will be great! Thank you.

Annabel puts the seat belt on Narnia.

Narnia
I want a cookie!

Annabel
Wait until your mum gets in.

Ash steps into the car. He shuts the door.

Ash
I must ring James and Toby when I get home.

Annabel
I have not spoken to them for a long time. How are they doing?

Ash
They fine.

Annabel sits down.

Annabel
I still remember what you three did before I left the school.

Ash
Do you?

Annabel
Yes,

Ash
What did we do?

Annabel
Befriending me when things turned nasty.

Ash
Nasty?

Annabel
With my ex.

Ash
Can I ask you a personal question?

Annabel
Sure.

Ash
What did you see in Chas?

Annabel
That is a good question.

Monica gets in the car.

Monica
Are you guys ready to go?

The three of them
Yes!

She closes the car door.

Monica
I may need to charge this car.

Ash
What percentage is it saying?

Monica
Do not worry.

Ash
Okay.

The car drives away.

Annabel to Ash
I noticed at the mall that your auntie's tummy was a little bit big. Is she pregnant?

Ash to Annabel
Yes.

Annabel
How many months is she?

Ash
4 months.

Annabel
Is she having a boy or a girl?

Ash
She's having twins.

Annabel
Twins?

Ash
Yes.

Annabel
Okay.

Ash
Would you like to have children in the future?

Annabel
It depends if my future husband wants them or not.

Ash
You don't have to let a man decide for you.

Annabel
What do you mean?

Ash
We live in an era that females have the power to choose whether to have family or not.

Annabel
I would like to have a family but at the same time, like to work.

Ash
As what?

Annabel
A Child and Teen therapist.
Ash
A Child and Teen therapist?

Annabel
Yes.

Ash
Okay. So ,you will be going to college then?

Annabel
Yes. What about you?

Ash
I have not decided.

Annabel
What are your grades?

Ash
Above average?

The car turns.

Monica
We are here.

Ash
Can we use the drive-in?

Monica
Do you want to dine?

Ash
No.

Monica
Alright.

The car goes over to the drive-in.

Man's voice on speaker
Hello, welcome to Wendy's! May I take your order?

Monica to the three of them
What would you all like?

Ash
Large chocolate milkshake, large fries, and a cheeseburger.

Annabel
Medium fries, medium diet coke, chicken burger and ice cream.

Monica
Okay.

Ash to Annabel
Are you doing anything at Christmas?

Annabel
Just spending it with family. What about you?

Ash
The same.

Annabel
I have an idea. How about we do something after Christmas?

Ash
That will be great

A woman at the window
Here are your orders, miss.

Monica
Thank you.

Woman
Enjoy.

Monica takes the bag along with the drinks and ice cream. Ash takes the bag. The car drives away.

ACT 6

Girl 4 to Girl 1
What's wrong with you?

Girl 1
I still can't stop thinking about those things I saw in Chas's car.

Girl 2 to Girl 1
Maybe a drink will calm your nerves.

A boy holding a bottle of beer comes over to the girls.

Boy
Enjoying the party?

Girl 3
Yes!

Boy to Girl 3
My name is Brad.

Girl 3
Kimberly.

Boy
Nice. My sister is also called Kimberly.

Girl 3
Is it?

Boy
Can I get you something to drink?

Girl 3
No, thank you.

Boy
Go on, just one or two?

Girl 3
Okay.

Boy
Be right back.

The boy walks away.

Girl 4 to Girl 3
You are letting a total stranger get you a drink?

Girl 3
He seems nice.

Girl 4 to Girl 3
Do you ever watch these teen crime dramas when a guy puts something in the girl's drink to make them pass out?

Girl 3 to Girl 4
Whatever do you mean?

The boy comes back.

Boy
There you go.

Girl 3
Sorry to be a pain but I just remembered that I'm driving.

Boy
You're driving?

Girl 3
Yes.

Boy
I see.

The boy walks away.

Girl 4
That's good.

A handsome man dress in a pilot's outfit approaches the four girls.

Man
Would you girls like a private viewing?

Girl 2
Of what?

Man
Seeing what I have got.

Girl 2
Alright.

Man
Meet me in the east wing guest room.

The four girls
Okay.

The man walks away.

Girl 1
I have not seen Caroline.

Girl 3
She's probably with Chas.

A shirtless Chas walks out from the bathroom. He walks over to a king-size bed.

Chas
Ready?

Caroline
Yes.

Chas
Start unzipping your dress?

Caroline
If you insist…

She begins unzipping her dress.

Chas
Can you be a little quicker!?

Caroline
I'm nervous!

Chas
Don't be!

The dress comes off.

Chas
Now, your bra and panties?

Caroline says nothing.

Chas
How can we make love?

Caroline
I need to go to the bathroom.

About the Characters

(ASH)

Ash is Tony's younger brother. He was only a week old when Monica's brother left him and Tony on the doorstep of Doncaster Mirandize's Georgian mansion in West Transylvania. At that time, Monica was just settling in with Doncaster and his father. Ash is close to his older brother along with his friends James, Toby, and Annabel, who the latter he worries the most due to her break up with older boyfriend. Ash is also intelligent and likes to read and write.

Lightning Source UK Ltd.
Milton Keynes UK
UKHW010633100621
385271UK00001B/112

9 781639 014415